MY SCHOOL
A PHOTOLOG BOOK

Created by Janet Horowitz and Kathy Faggella

Illustrated by Steve Jenkins

Stewart, Tabori & Chang
New York

Published in 1991 by
Stewart, Tabori & Chang, Inc.
575 Broadway, New York, New York 10012

Distributed in the U.S. by Workman Publishing,
708 Broadway, New York, New York 10003
Distributed in Canada by Canadian Manda Group,
P.O. Box 920 Station U, Toronto, Ontario M8Z 5P9
Distributed in all other territories by
Little, Brown and Company, International Division,
34 Beacon Street, Boston, Massachusetts 02108

Printed in Singapore
10 9 8 7 6 5 4 3 2

School is a large part of your life. School is not only a place to learn, but it's a place to meet friends and get involved in fun events. Each one of your school years is different. Each one is very special. Your classmates, your teachers, your best friends are important to you. So . . . this book's for you! Take pictures, interview friends, teachers, and classmates; collect autographs, and keep it all right here. You can be a photographer, reporter, and writer of your own PhotoLog book about you and your school.

Uses for your **My School** book:

- Use **My School** to have fun with your friends and to collect their autographs.

- Use **My School** to capture your feelings, opinions and reactions to all the happenings in your year at school.

- Use **My School** to help you take a look at your school in a new way, and learn new things about it.

- Use **My School** as a conversation piece with your friends and family. Compare and share this information with them.

- Use **My School** as an example of the pride you feel for your school and share it with visitors and newcomers.

- Use **My School** as a treasured memory book, to help you remember all the special times you've had in your school.

Some hints to help you complete your book:

1. Take photos.
You will need one roll of 24-print film to complete this book. Take all the photos yourself, or ask someone to take a few so that you can be in them. Use the photo captions in this book to suggest the pictures to take. You may want to show this book to people you are photographing so that they know why you are taking their picture.

2. Talk with your classmates and teachers.
Use this book as a way to make new friends and to better understand old ones. You may want to ask questions or interview people. You can also listen carefully to what people say and watch what they do.

3. Fill in this book.
When your photos are ready, decide which ones best fit the photo captions and pages of this book. Complete the fill-ins at any time, by yourself or with the person that the page is about. Let classmates autograph the special pages with names, verses, and doodles. Follow the order in this book, or skip around. You do not have to fill in everything. And remember, have fun!

My full name is

Mariah Simone Gardner

I am _____ years old.

My favorite:

Hobby _____   Song _____

TV show _____   Singer _____

Sport _____   Book _____

Color _____   Food _____

Movie _____   Star _____

School name:_____,

address: _____.

The best place to be in school is _____

_____.

The worst place to have to be is _____

_____.

My favorite room is _____

_____.

My desk is ☐ very neat ☐ sometimes neat ☐ sloppy

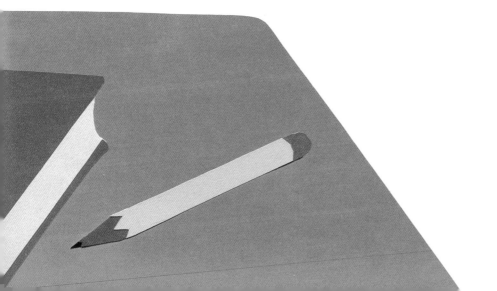

I sit next to _____.

My favorite spot in the classroom is_____

_____.

If I could change anything about my classroom, I would

_____.

Our class pet is _____.

The best note passer is _____.

The best talker is _____.

The best gum chewer without being noticed is_____
_____. The best excuse maker for not having
homework in on time is _____.

The funniest is_____.

A classmate who can make an angry teacher laugh is ____
_____. The classmate who goes to the
nurse most often is _____.

My best friend's name is

I call my best friend _____.

The things we like to do together are _____

_____

_____.

The things that make my best friend happiest are_____

_____.

My best friend's autograph:

_____.

MY BEST FRIEND

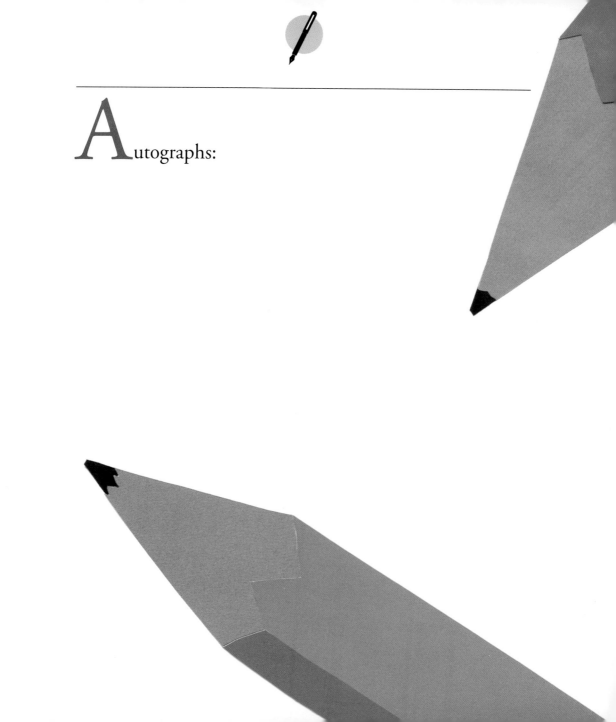

A utographs:

GREAT KIDS IN MY CLASS

More autographs:

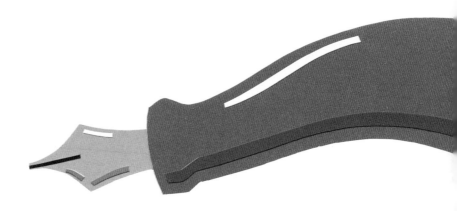

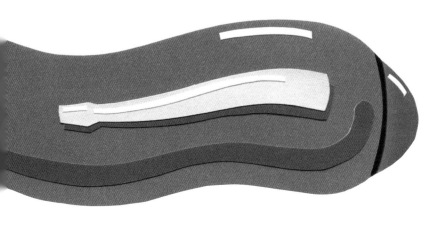

S chool starts at  [fill in hands]

At that time you can find me:

☐ still eating
   breakfast
☐ sharpening
   pencils

☐ writing the first
   note of the day
☐ finishing my
   homework
☐ chatting

☐ at my desk
☐ in the
   bathroom
☐ starting lunch

Free time is at _____

and I'm usually_____

_____ .

A PICTURE OF ME AT SCHOOL

My teacher's name is _____.

The class calls my teacher _____.

My teacher's favorite expression is _____

_____.

My teacher loves to _____.

If I were the teacher, I would _____.

I would never _____.

MY TEACHER

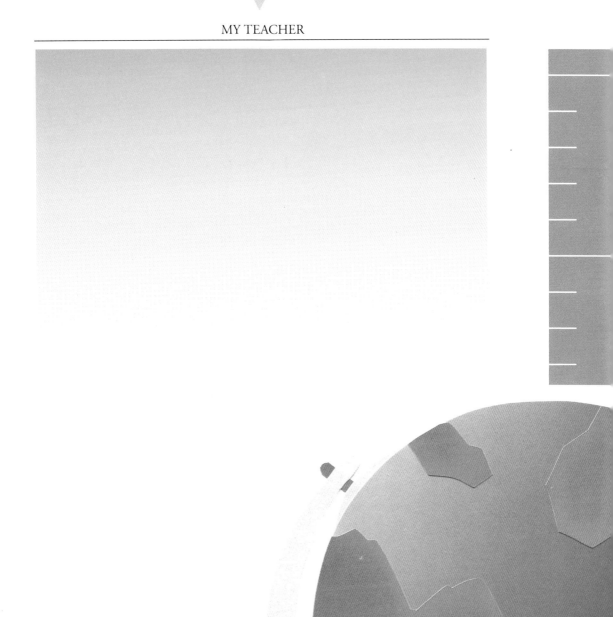

Teachers in our school:

the snobbiest _____

the funniest _____

the best dressed _____

the worst dressed _____

the nicest _____

the toughest _____

the easiest to talk to _____

the yeller _____

the talker _____

the teacher who gives the most homework assignments

_____.

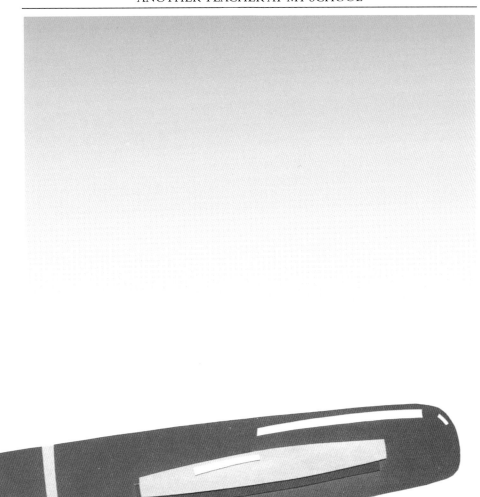

Principal _____

☐ Vice principal _____

☐ My counselor _____

☐ A favorite secretary _____

☐ School nurse _____

☐ Librarian _____

☐ School guard _____

☐ other _____

Check the person you see most often.

Double check the person you like the most.

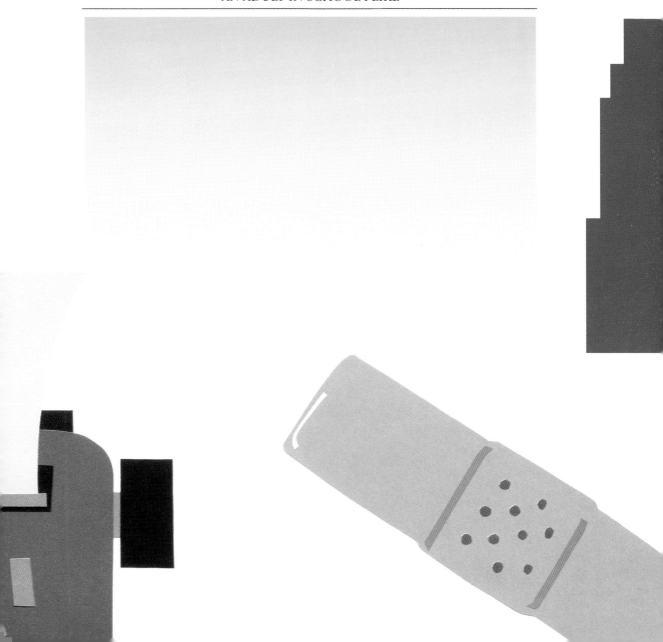

For lunch I usually:

- ☐ bring something from home
- ☐ buy something
- ☐ switch with a friend
- ☐ eat part of a friend's lunch
- ☐ starve
- ☐ eat the best snacks
- ☐ sleep
- ☐ dump it
- ☐ have nothing left of my lunch to eat
- ☐ _____

The greatest lunch I ever brought from home was _____
_____.

The worst school lunch I ever had was _____
_____.

My favorite school lunch is _____.

The kid with the best lunches is _____.

If I were running the cafeteria I'd sell _____
_____.

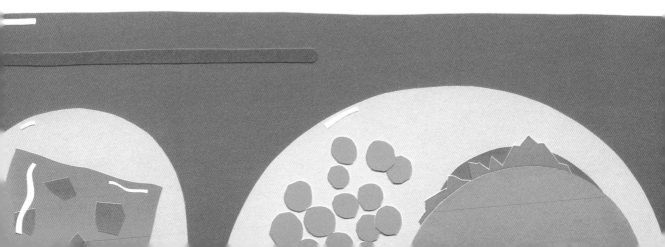

Schooll ends at  [fill in hands]

At this time you can find me:

☐ going home with a friend
☐ off to another activity
☐ waiting to be picked up by
_____

☐ talking with the principal
☐ cleaning up
☐ rushing home to call friends

☐ passing the last note of the day
☐ other
_____

Things I do after school are _____
_____.

The kids I'm usually with are _____
_____.

I like this activity because _____
_____.

My dream after-school activity would be to _____
_____.

A PICTURE OF ME AT AN AFTER-SCHOOL ACTIVITY

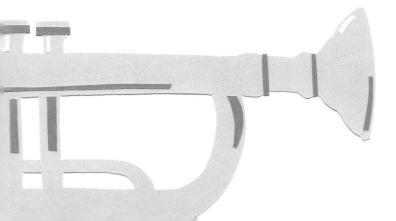

The funniest thing that happened at school was when
_____.

The silliest thing that happened this year was _____
_____.

The most embarrassing thing that happened was _____
_____.

This photo is a picture of when _____
_____.

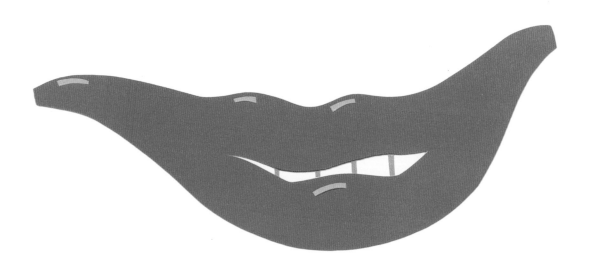

A FUN TIME

Our class took a trip to _____

_____.

To get there we had to _____

_____.

One thing I really learned was _____

_____.

For my next trip I'd like to

_____

_____.

Events our school had this year were:

- ☐ concert
- ☐ fair/carnival
- ☐ school play
- ☐ talent show

- ☐ open-house program
- ☐ field day
- ☐ a special visitor

- ☐ sale (kind)
  _____
- ☐ other
  _____

The event I enjoyed the most was _____

because _____

_____.

AT A SPECIAL EVENT

_____

School News:

the "hottest" clothing style _____

coolest jewelry _____

neatest game _____

most popular slang words _____

the biggest secret _____

_____

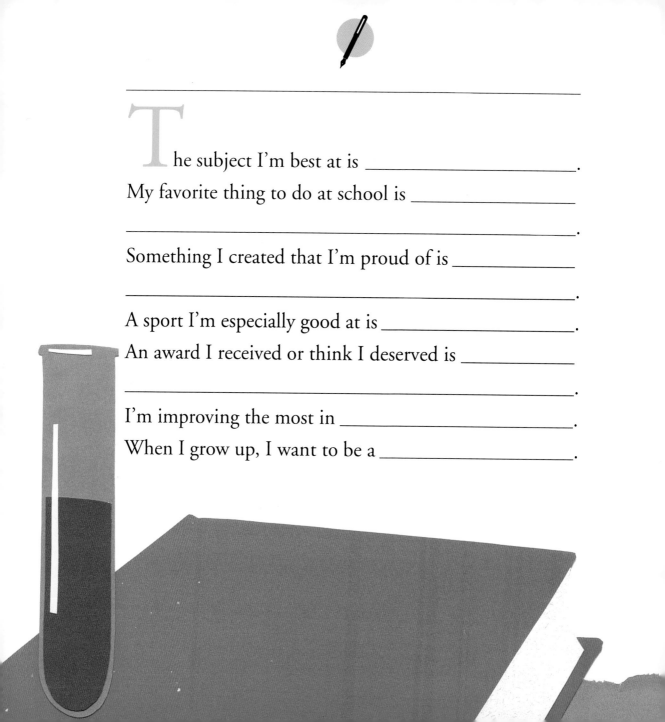

The subject I'm best at is _____.

My favorite thing to do at school is _____

_____.

Something I created that I'm proud of is _____

_____.

A sport I'm especially good at is _____.

An award I received or think I deserved is _____

_____.

I'm improving the most in _____.

When I grow up, I want to be a _____.

M y summer plans are _____

_____

_____.

Important addresses to remember:

_____

_____

_____

F

ill in this report card the way you'd like to see it:

Subject   Grade

_____   _____

_____   _____

_____   _____

_____   _____

Conduct: _____

Comments:_____

_____

_____

Tardy _____ Absences _____ Promoted to _____

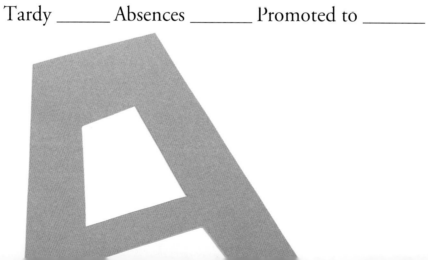

A FAVORITE PHOTO

Paste your report card here or fill it in with any extra photos, souvenirs, or notes you wish to save.

Design by Jenkins & Page, New York, NY.
Art Photography by Gamma One Conversions, New York, NY.
Composed in Adobe Garamond.
Type proofs by Graphic Arts Composition, Philadelphia, PA.
Printed and bound by Toppan Printing Company, Ltd., Singapore.